POKIE PETUNIA

Lynda Zidanic

tate publishing
CHILDREN'S DIVISION

Published by Tate Publishing & Enterprises, LLC
127 E. Trade Center Terrace | Mustang, Oklahoma 73064 USA
1.888.361.9473 | www.tatepublishing.com

Tate Publishing is committed to excellence in the publishing industry. The company reflects the philosophy established by the founders, based on Psalm 68:11,
"The Lord gave the word and great was the company of those who published it."

Book design copyright © 2016 by Tate Publishing, LLC. All rights reserved.
Cover and interior design by Rhezette Fiel
Illustrations by Bea May Ybanez

Published in the United States of America

ISBN: 978-1-68352-606-3
1. Juvenile Fiction / Animals / General
2. Juvenile Fiction / Social Themes / Self-Esteem & Self-Reliance
16.06.08

This book is dedicated to my niece Sadie who
has overcome many challenges in her life.

Long ago in the Bewilderment Forest lived a little turtle named Petunia. Petunia wasn't like the other animal children in the forest. She was slow. So the other animal children gave her the nickname Pokie Petunia.

One day while the animal children were whispering and laughing, Petunia slowly came up to them and said, "Good morning". The animal children smiled and said, "Good morning Petunia."

When they thought Petunia was out
of hearing range they continued
on laughing and talking about her.
Unfortunately, she overheard them and
dashed off into the forest.

When Petunia knew she was alone, she crawled into her shell and started to cry. While crying she said, "I can't believe they were making fun of me all this time, I thought they were my friends."

Just then Petunia heard, rat-a-tat-tat, on the side of her shell. It was her teacher Mrs. Owl. "What is wrong my dear, why are you crying?"

"Oh Mrs. Owl, none of the children like me. They make fun of me and call me names. They call me, Pokie Petunia, because I am so slow."

"My sweet little Petunia, you may be slow, but you do things well. You put a lot of care in the things you do. As for the other animal children who have been making fun of you, they have been careless in their schoolwork. Making simple mistakes they could have avoided, simply by taking their time, and checking over their work.

Just then, Sammy the squirrel came calling out, "Mrs. Owl help! I need you! Please help get these burrs out of my fluffy tail." Mrs. Owl replied, "I have some papers to finish checking, maybe Petunia can help you."

Sammy said, "How about it Petunia, will you please help me by taking these burrs out of my tail? I know I haven't been very nice to you and for that I am truly sorry." Petunia thought for a brief moment and said, "Okay, I will help you."

By the end of lunch Sammy's tail was burr free. "Thanks for helping me, that feels ssssoooo much better." The rest of the animal children joined Sammy and Petunia. They asked Petunia to forgive them for teasing her. She said, "yes" and they lived happily ever after.

⊖|LIVE

listen|imagine|view|experience

AUDIO BOOK DOWNLOAD INCLUDED WITH THIS BOOK!

In your hands you hold a complete digital entertainment package. In addition to the paper version, you receive a free download of the audio version of this book. Simply use the code listed below when visiting our website. Once downloaded to your computer, you can listen to the book through your computer's speakers, burn it to an audio CD or save the file to your portable music device (such as Apple's popular iPod) and listen on the go!

How to get your free audio book digital download:

1. Visit www.tatepublishing.com and click on the eILIVE logo on the home page.
2. Enter the following coupon code:
   0412-06f8-e2b8-4e6a-7b70-1788-fe8c-10ce
3. Download the audio book from your eILIVE digital locker and begin enjoying your new digital entertainment package today!

Geri,

May the Lord bless you extra special for all your kindness you show to _all_ you meet.

You are such a pleasure to see in the A.M.

Love,
Lynda Zidavic

CPSIA information can be obtained at www.ICGtesting.com
Printed in the USA
BVOW05s0000280716

456955BV00002B/4/P